BLACK ADAM

AN ORIGIN STORY

raintree
a Capstone company — publishers for children

Raintree is an imprint of Capstone Global Library Limited, a company incorporated in England and Wales having its registered office at 264 Banbury Road, Oxford, OX2 7DY – Registered company number: 6695582

www.raintree.co.uk
myorders@raintree.co.uk

Designed by Hilary Wacholz
Originated by Capstone Global Library Ltd

978 1 3982 4440 5 (hardback)
978 1 3982 4439 9 (paperback)

British Library Cataloguing in Publication Data
A full catalogue record for this book is available from the British Library.

Printed and bound in India

SUPER
-VILLAINS

BLACK ADAM

AN ORIGIN STORY

WRITTEN BY
MATTHEW K. MANNING

ILLUSTRATED BY
DARIO BRIZUELA

It's hard to believe that Black Adam was ever a hero.

But a very long time ago, he was.

In the 13th century, in a country called Kahndaq, Black Adam is known as Teth-Adam. He might just be the bravest hero the world has ever seen.

Teth-Adam is the son of royalty. But he spends his time helping those with far less. Almost every day, he saves a life.

Adam protects the helpless. He takes food to families in need. He does good deeds even when no one is watching.

But really, someone has been paying close attention. Someone watches Teth-Adam from the shadows.

One night, Teth-Adam is called to the chambers of the most powerful person in all of Kahndaq. This man is the Wizard called Shazam.
He controls strange, ancient magic.

"Step forward," says the Wizard.

Teth-Adam is in awe of the mighty figure. So he does not speak.
He simply does as he is told.

The Wizard points his staff at Adam.

"For your great deeds, you have been chosen to bear my magic," the Wizard says. "Say my name, and it will be yours."

"Shazam!" says Teth-Adam.

Suddenly, a bolt of magical lightning shoots down from above. It strikes the hero.

KRAKOW!!!

When the smoke clears, a very different man stands before the Wizard.

"What . . . what have you done to me?" asks Teth-Adam.

"You are no longer just a man," says the Wizard. "Now, you are a warrior for justice. A protector of the powerless."

Again, Teth-Adam says nothing. Too many thoughts swirl in his mind.

"You are the world's champion," says the Wizard. "And we will call you . . . Mighty Adam."

The Wizard's lightning grants Mighty Adam the powers of ancient gods.

From the god Shu, Mighty Adam gains stamina. He does not grow tired. He can use his powers for hours without stopping.

From the great Heru, he earns
swiftness. Mighty Adam can run
and fly at super-speed!

The god Amon grants Mighty Adam
incredible strength. Adam is much
stronger than a normal human.

Great Zehuti gives Mighty Adam wisdom. The hero can solve any problem. He just needs to think about it hard enough.

The god Aton lends his pure power to Mighty Adam. The hero crackles with magical energy.

And finally, the god Mehen grants great courage to the hero. Teth-Adam was always bold. But Mighty Adam's bravery knows no limit.

Year after year, Mighty Adam serves his country. He uses his powers to save countless lives. He helps countless people.

But great power can also corrupt.

After some time, Mighty Adam begins to see people as weak and afraid. He finds it a chore to come to their rescue.

"Why serve these sheep when I can rule as a lion?" Mighty Adam asks himself.

With those words, he steps away from the noble path of the Wizard.

People stop calling him Mighty Adam. He is Khem-Adam now. It is a name that matches his dark heart.

It means Black Adam.

But the Wizard can't allow Black Adam to be so selfish. Adam was not meant to rule over his people. He was meant to help them.

To punish Black Adam for his crimes, the Wizard uses nearly all his magical power. With a spell, he traps Black Adam's soul in an amulet.

There Adam stays for hundreds of years.

Then one day, a man called Theo Adam is exploring ancient ruins in Kahndaq. He finds the old amulet.

With a touch, he sets Black Adam free.

But Black Adam has learned nothing from his time locked away. He is angry. He only wants revenge!

It's not long before Black Adam finds out the Wizard chose a new hero to protect this modern world.

"I am the Wizard's champion!" he growls with rage. "No one is fit to hold that title but me."

Black Adam flies into the sky.
He soon arrives halfway across the
world in a place called Fawcett City.

"Show yourself, false champion!"
he shouts.

No one answers.

Even angrier than before, Black Adam lashes out. He rips the sign off the WHIZ radio station building.

RRRRRRENCH!

He hurls the sign at the crowded street below. The heavy metal flies right towards a city bus!

WHOOOOSH!!!

Suddenly a man grabs the sign in mid-air. He crackles with lightning.

He is Shazam, the Wizard's new champion.

This Super Hero also has the power of the gods. The wisdom of Solomon! The strength of Hercules! The stamina of Atlas! The power of Zeus! The courage of Achilles! And the speed of Mercury!

Shazam gently places the sign down and turns to face his new foe.

Black Adam charges forward with his fist.

THOCK!

"Imposter!" Black Adam yells.

"I don't even know who you are!" says Shazam, stumbling back.

"I am the Wizard's real champion!" says Black Adam.

He swings his fist again.

WHUMP!

But this time, Shazam uses the speed of Mercury to catch Adam's hand.

"I am the chosen one!" Black Adam shouts.

He uses all his strength. He forces Shazam to his knee.

"I am the Wizard's true hero!" screams Black Adam.

"This . . . ," Shazam says, "this is how you think a hero behaves?"

For the third time in his life, Black Adam is left without words.

He backs away from Shazam. He looks at the scared people all around them.

The people fear me, thinks Black Adam. *They see me as some . . . monster.*

Then Adam flies off in a flash. He doesn't stop until he is back in Kahndaq.

In his homeland, Black Adam makes a promise. "I will earn my title," he says. "I will be the Wizard's true champion once again."

And perhaps he means it. Maybe he will make up for his past mistakes.

But for those with the wisdom of Solomon . . . it remains hard to believe.

BLACK ADAM

REAL NAME: TETH-ADAM
CRIMINAL NAME: BLACK ADAM
ROLE: SUPER-VILLAIN
BASE: KAHNDAQ

Black Adam claims to be the greatest hero in the world. However, Super Hero Shazam knows better. Teth-Adam gained his abilities from the same Wizard as Shazam. But the power went to Teth-Adam's head. Now called Black Adam, the villain often strays from a noble path for his own gain. No matter how great his power, Black Adam always hungers for more.

THE AUTHOR

MATTHEW K. MANNING has written dozens of comics and books starring Batman, Superman, Wonder Woman, Cyborg, Green Lantern, The Flash and even Scooby-Doo. Some of his favourites include the comic book crossover Batman/Teenage Mutant Ninja Turtles Adventures, the IDW comic Marvel Action: Avengers and the Capstone chapter book series Xander and the Rainbow-Barfing Unicorns. He lives in North Carolina, USA, with his wife, Dorothy, and his two daughters, Lillian and Gwendolyn.

THE ILLUSTRATOR

DARIO BRIZUELA works traditionally and digitally in many different illustration styles. His work can be found in a wide range of properties, including Star Wars Tales, DC Super Hero Girls, DC Super Friends, Transformers, Scooby-Doo! Team-Up and more. Brizuela lives in Buenos Aires, Argentina.

GLOSSARY

amulet piece of jewellery that has magical powers to protect against evil

champion someone who fights for a person, group or cause

corrupt cause something good to become bad and evil

imposter person who lies to others by pretending to be someone else

noble having to do with what is right and good

revenge act of harming someone because they harmed you

stamina energy to keep doing something for a long time

swiftness being very quick and fast

wisdom knowledge, good judgment and the ability to understand

wizard person, often a man, with magical powers

DISCUSSION QUESTIONS

Write down your answers. Look back at the story for help.

QUESTION 1.

Why do you think the Wizard chose Teth-Adam to be his champion? What makes someone a true hero?

QUESTION 2.

Why do you think Black Adam turned evil? Was the Wizard right to trap him in the amulet? Explain your answer.

QUESTION 3.

Do you think one day Black Adam could be a hero again? Explain why or why not.

QUESTION 4.

What is your favourite illustration in this book? Explain your choice.

READ THEM ALL!!

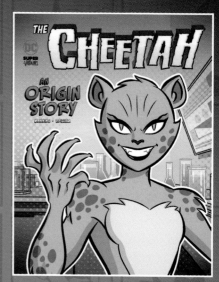